Wisdom Publications
199 Elm Street
Somerville, MA 02144 USA
wisdomexperience.org

Library of Congress Cataloging-in-Publication Data
Names: MacLean, Kerry Lee, author.
Title: A peaceful piggy's guide to sickness and death, sadness and love /
Kerry Lee MacLean.
Description: Somerville, MA: Wisdom Publications, [2022] |
Audience: Grades 2–3. |
Identifiers: LCCN 2021024491 (print) | LCCN 2021024492 (ebook) |
ISBN 9781614297819 (hardcover) | ISBN 9781614298038 (ebook)
Subjects: CYAC: Mindfulness (Psychology)—Fiction. | Meditation—Fiction. |
Death—Fiction. | Pigs—Fiction. | LCGFT: Picture books.
Classification: LCC PZ7.M22436 Ph 2022 (print) | LCC PZ7.M22436 (ebook) |
DDC [E]—dc23
LC record available at https://lccn.loc.gov/2021024491
LC ebook record available at https://lccn.loc.gov/2021024492

ISBN 978-1-61429-781-9
ebook ISBN 978-1-61429-803-8

26 25 24 23 22   5 4 3 2 1

Cover and interior design by Katrina Damkoehler.

Printed on acid-free paper that meets the guidelines for permanence and
durability of the Production Guidelines for Book Longevity of the Council on Library Resources.

Printed in Malaysia.

A PEACEFUL PIGGY'S GUIDE TO SICKNESS AND DEATH, SADNESS AND LOVE

Kerry Lee MacLean

Wisdom

Dedicated to Manjushri
and, always and forever, my grandchildren:

For you, Eloise, Lucy, and Colin!
You've lived with sick family members your whole lives
and have become so very kind because of it. And thank you,
thank you, nine-year-old Eloise, for editing this book like a pro
and pitching some really great ideas! Thank you also to my
wonderful editors, Laura Cunningham and Brianna Quick,
for their kind and skillful guidance.

WHEN SOMEONE WE LOVE
GETS SICK

When someone we love gets sick, we little piggies worry! It might feel scary when a person we care about is sick in bed or when they're stuck in the hospital and we can't even visit them!

Luckily, there is one good thing we peaceful piggies can do: meditate. Mindful breathing calms us. Just sitting peacefully makes us feel better.

Our peaceful piggy peacefulness makes our loved ones feel better, too.

No matter how close or far away they are!

Mindful Walking

If we just CAN'T sit calmly, we can walk mindfully instead of sitting. Walking very *s l o w l y* in a circle, we feel our feet pressing down onto the ground, then lifting up and swinging through the air, then pressing down again into the ground. Over and over, around and around, this gives a peaceful feeling inside.

Sky Meditation

When we lie on the ground or the floor like a starfish, look out into the sky, and feel our breath, we feel safe with strong Mother Earth holding us up. Big Father Sky makes our thoughts disappear like the imprint of a bird in the sky.

After a few minutes of mindfulness we feel . . . *"Aahhh . . ."*
We send that *"Aahhh . . ."* to the one we love, and they smile.

WHEN SOMEONE WE LOVE
IS DYING

When a person we love is dying, sometimes our mom or dad or another grown-up helps us cut flowers and leaves, or buy silk ones, to make a special kind of flower arrangement to remind them we love them.

Zen Flower Meditation

The heaven leaves point up to the sky.
The earth leaves point down to the earth.
The flowers go in the middle. They are our love.

You know your flower arrangement is done when it makes you feel calm just looking at it.

When a person we love is dying, we might say, "No! But we don't want you to go! We'll miss you."

"When you miss me, close your eyes, breathe in, and breathe out; breathing makes you feel better. Then put your hand on your heart. Feel the warmth in there? That's me, loving you."

And when someone we love is dying,
we peaceful piggies might ask, "Where
will you go when you leave your body?"

"I hope I go to heaven."

"What's heaven?"

"Heaven is high up in the clouds,
where I can look down and watch over you."

Or we might ask, "If you could come back and be born as anything you want, what would you be?" And they might look out the window at the squirrels pouncing and bouncing through the trees and say, "I think I'd like to be a squirrel."

"A squirrel?! Why?"

"Because squirrels always seem so happy. They chase each other, running through the grass and jumping from branch to branch, playing together all day long."

And we look out the window and smile.

WHEN SOMEONE WE LOVE

HAS DIED

Meditation with the Mind Jar

We take turns putting our sparkly thoughts in the water of the Mind Jar. Sad thoughts, angry feelings, and scary ideas float together with loving thoughts and even some happy thoughts.

We stir up the jar and a crazy tornado of feelings forms, whirling faster and faster.

Then, we ring the gong.

"Goooooonnnnngggg"

We sit up straight and just breathe, in and out. In . . . out . . . in . . . out . . . watching our mad, sad, and worried thoughts twirl slower and slower beside our loving and happy feelings. And we just let all those mixed-up feelings *be*.

Some sparkles sink down to the bottom,
and some rise up to the top.
The tornado of feelings is gone
and we feel calm and clear,
just like the water
in the Mind Jar.

We feel calm.

We feel peaceful.

And now we know how to let the person we love go. When our mind is settled and clear, we can feel the love in our heart and we can just . . . let go.

Like watching a bubble rise up, up, and away, so high in the sky that we can't even see it anymore. We say, "Goodbye. We love you!"

When the person we love dies,
we peaceful piggies sometimes wonder,

"Where are they going?"

"What will they do there?"

"I hope it's someplace good!"

"I hope they're happy!"

"Me, too!"

"I hope they feel all the love
I have for them in my heart."

We think about how much
we love them . . .

and we smile.

And even though they're gone, like magic we still see them everywhere. The stars are their shining eyes and the moon is our loved one smiling back at us.

Dear parents, teachers, therapists, and every other grown-up,

This is a story of hope. It helps to calm and empower anxious children when they understand that they can still be with their loved ones through their heart connection, even if their loved one is sick, dying, or has passed on. Nurturing their living heart connection with mindfulness exercises soothes their troubled spirits. Kids will no longer feel completely powerless when they're able to actively send feelings of peace, calm, and loving-kindness to their loved ones. The pages that follow will give you practical instructions for the meditation activities mentioned in this book. Rather than approaching death as a morbid or taboo topic, we can help kids cope best by gently presenting life just as it is. I hope the tools in this book will be useful supports to you and the children in your life, as you guide them through this challenging time.

All the love in the world!
KERRY LEE MACLEAN

A LITTLE MORE ABOUT THESE MINDFULNESS PRACTICES

Practicing mindful breathing with children, I was truly surprised to discover that where it takes me an hour to settle my mind, children only need five minutes! I guess this may be because their minds are more fluid and flexible than most adults', and children naturally reside more in the present moment. With each of these meditations, start with just one minute and add one more minute each week until you get up to five (ten for teens). Begin and end each session by ringing a gong or bell. Hit the ending gong as hard as you can, then whisper, "Raise your hand when you can't hear the sound of the gong anymore." As they quietly focus so intently on their sense of hearing, their awareness of the present moment intensifies and the sense of peace in the room can be amazing.

Sitting Meditation

The practice is to simply sit quietly together, cross-legged in an upright posture, as we follow the natural rhythm of the breath. As thoughts and sometimes overwhelming feelings arise, instead of following that train of thought, we let it go by placing our attention back on the breath, which pulls us out of our heads and into the freshness of the present moment. This builds a child's "letting go" muscles. This practice might be challenging if you're feeling sad, but it's important to keep the atmosphere light, loving, and supportive.

Walking Meditation

This walking meditation comes from the Japanese practice of Zen, where walking breaks are interspersed with sitting meditation. The body should be relaxed with hands held loosely over the diaphragm, one palm over a loose fist. The walk should be slow and relaxed, like a pleasant stroll. Instead of following the breath, we pay attention to the sensations of our feet swinging through the air, pressing down into the ground, lifting, swinging, pressing; calmly moving through space. It's great if it can be done outdoors!

Sky Meditation

The sky meditation is pretty self-explanatory. The important thing to grasp is that any experience of spaciousness is soothing to a child's riled mind. Simply being outside in nature, or going for a walk, is calming; gazing up into the sky is the ultimate experience of space.

Flower Meditation

Begin with a one-minute sitting meditation. This flower meditation is a simplified form of Japan's ancient contemplative art of ikebana, which creates harmony by bringing heaven, earth, and the human or heart element together. The tallest branch, leaves, or grass bring in heaven, or awareness of space, while the lower leaves, ivy, bark, moss, or rocks bring a sense of ground, or earth. The flowers in the middle are our heart, binding heaven and earth. It can be a wonderful adult-child activity that instantly brings calm and a feeling of harmony into the home and the heart. If the flower arrangement can be sent or given to the loved one who is ill, it can be meaningful for both the giver and the receiver.

I got the idea for the Mind Jar from a demonstration of a Zen teaching technique, where the teacher dumped a handful of dirt into a glass of water, telling us the clear water was our mind and the dirt was our thoughts. He stirred it up and we all sat mesmerized as the dirt slowly sank to the bottom and the glass of water cleared (mostly). For children, I substituted the dirt with different colored sparkles for different thoughts and feelings, in order to help them become more aware of all that arises in their minds, and how transitory it all is. We just sit and let our thoughts and feelings be. In times of great stress, anxiety, grief, fear, and depression, daily Mind Jar meditation helps children to self-settle and self-reflect, to articulate their feelings and let them go again and again—gradually self-healing their trauma so they can more easily regain their natural balance and eventually live their lives in a healthier, happier way. (For a "greener" way to do the Mind Jar, biodegradable sparkles are available on Amazon.)

ABOUT THE AUTHOR

KERRY LEE MACLEAN started daily meditation at the age of fourteen and eventually meditated daily (sort of) with her husband and five children. Seeing the amazing benefits of families regularly stopping for a peaceful moment together, Kerry then dedicated her life to starting a worldwide family meditation movement. In addition to writing her books, she has taught her Mind Jar in hundreds of elementary schools and led family meditative arts days, rites-of-passage programs, and teacher trainings internationally for thirty-five years, often together with her husband and three of her now-adult daughters. She is the author of ten books, including *Peaceful Piggy Meditation*, *Moody Cow Meditates*, and *The Family Meditation Book*—an expanded edition of which is in the works. She's also the illustrator of *Peaceful Piggy Bedtime*, which is by her daughter Sophie Maclaren, and *Mindful Monkey, Happy Panda* by Lauren Alderfer. These days Kerry spends most of her time happily playing with her grandchildren! For free downloads, go to kerrymaclean.com. Kerry loves corresponding with her readers at kerryleemaclean@gmail.com.